For my children with all my love

First published in Great Britain in November 2016 by Bloomsbury Publishing Plc
Published in the United States of America in August 2017
by Bloomsbury Children's Books
www.bloomsbury.com

Bloomsbury is a registered trademark of Bloomsbury Publishing Plc

For information about permission to reproduce selections from this book, write to
Permissions, Bloomsbury Children's Books, 1385 Broadway, New York, New York 10018
Bloomsbury books may be purchased for business or promotional use. For information on bulk purchases please contact
Macmillan Corporate and Premium Sales Department at specialmarkets@macmillan.com

Library of Congress Cataloging-in-Publication Data
Names: Gliori, Debi, author, illustrator.
Title: Goodnight world / by Debi Gliori.
Description: New York : Bloomsbury, 2017.
Summary: Join in the list of important things to say goodnight to—ships, animals, plants, toys, and, of course, the sun.
Identifiers: LCCN 2016037880
ISBN 978-1-68119-363-2 (hardcover) • ISBN 978-1-68119-717-3 (e-book) • ISBN 978-1-68119-716-6 (e-PDF)
Subjects: | CYAC: Stories in rhyme. | Bedtime—Fiction. | BISAC: JUVENILE FICTION / Bedtime & Dreams. |
JUVENILE FICTION / Animals / General. | JUVENILE FICTION / Family / General (see also headings under Social Issues).
Classification: LCC PZ8.3.G47 Go 2017 | DDC [E]—dc23
LC record available at https://lccn.loc.gov/2016037880

Art created with charcoal and watercolor
Typeset in a font created from the author's hand lettering
Book design by Zoe Waring
Printed in China by C & C Offset Printing Co., Ltd., Shenzhen, Guangdong
2 4 6 8 10 9 7 5 3 1

All papers used by Bloomsbury Publishing, Inc., are natural, recyclable products made from wood grown in well-managed forests.
The manufacturing processes conform to the environmental regulations of the country of origin.

Goodnight
World

Debi Gliori

BLOOMSBURY

NEW YORK LONDON OXFORD NEW DELHI SYDNEY

Goodnight planet,
goodnight world.
Peaceful clouds
around Earth curled.

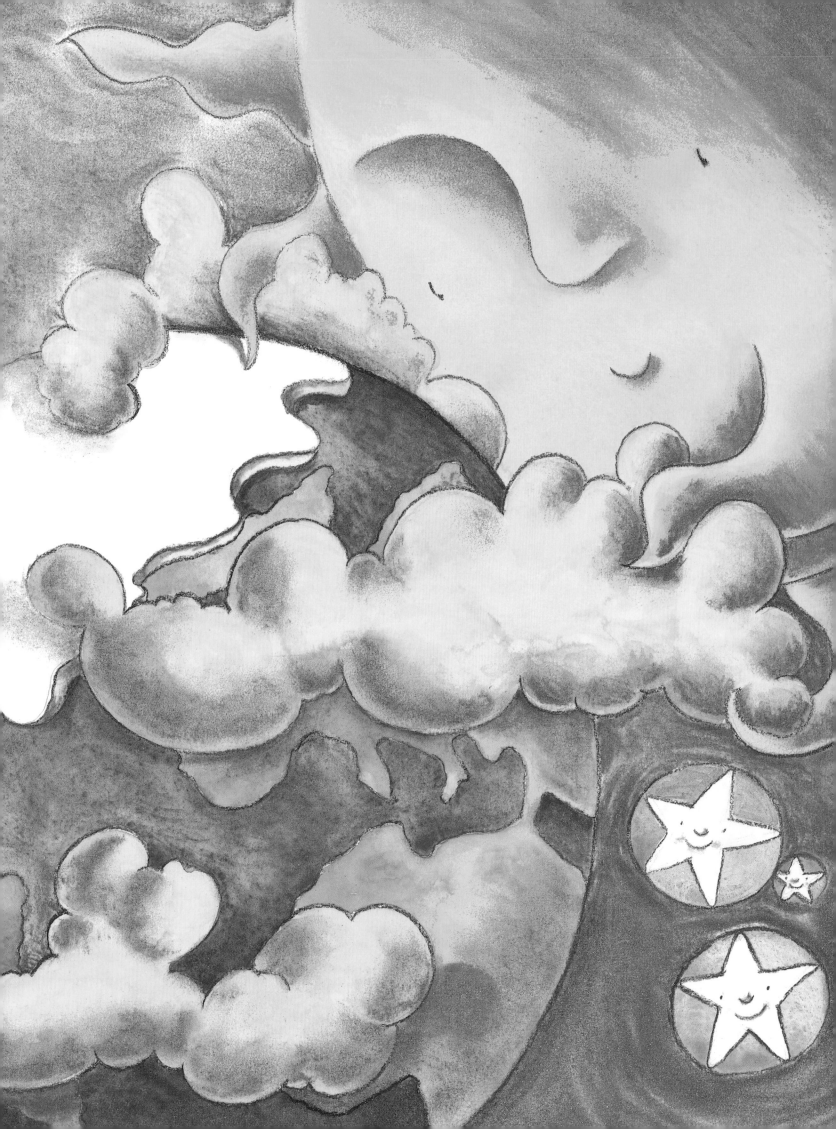

Goodnight ice and goodnight snow.

Goodnight lights above, aglow.

Goodnight oceans
deep and wide,

rocking ships
upon the tide.

Goodnight trucks
and cars and planes.

Goodnight rockets,
goodnight trains.

Goodnight birds,
goodnight bees.

Goodnight fishes
in the seas.

Goodnight flowers,
goodnight grasses

curled up tight
while darkness passes.

Goodnight lions,
tigers, too,
and all the animals
in the zoo.

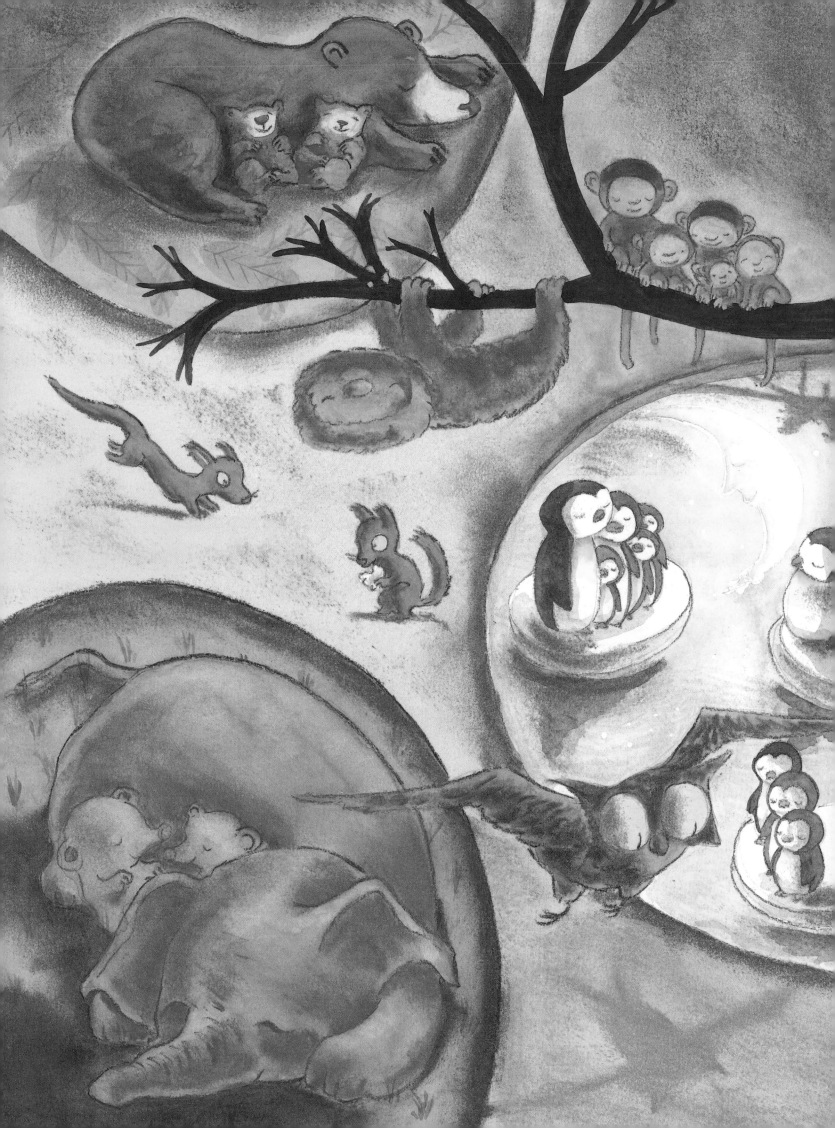

Goodnight shadows
in the park.

Goodnight dog
that doesn't bark.

Goodnight teddies,
goodnight books.
Goodnight sparrows,
starlings, rooks.

Goodnight sounds
of distant cars,
and in the sky,
a million stars.

Goodnight moon,
goodnight sun.
Goodnight, goodnight,
to everyone.

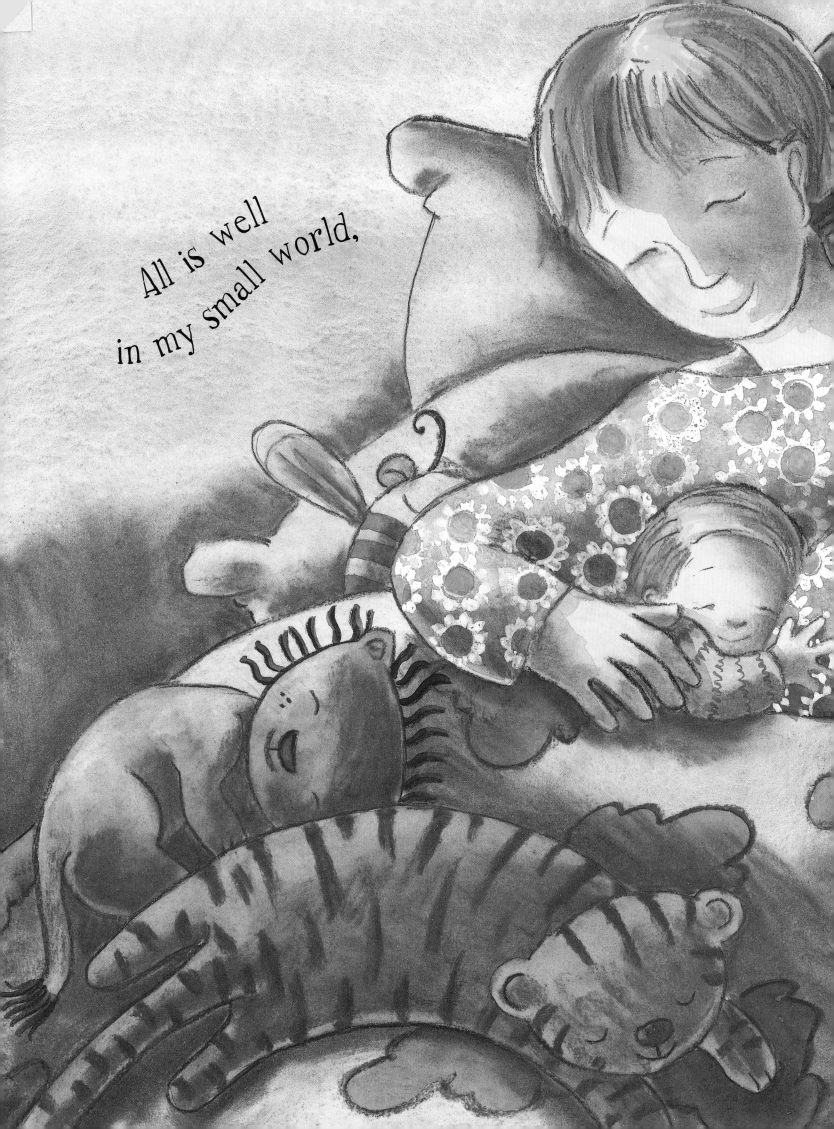

All is well
in my small world,

around my mother's heart
I'm curled.